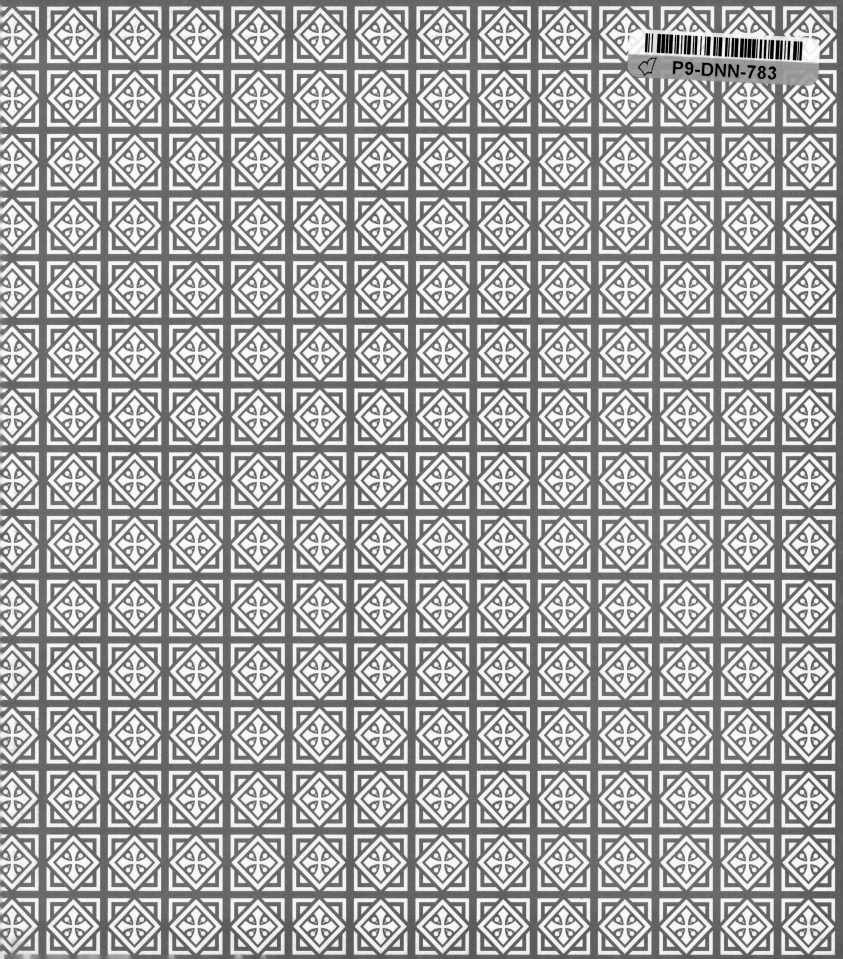

Michael Hague's Magical World of Unicorns

To Dr. Harry Anderson

Reasonable efforts have been made to contact the authors of certain material quoted in this work. Authors who the publisher was unable to locate should contact the publisher at the address indicated, and we will be happy to make the necessary correction in future printings. Some of the selections were taken from works of public domain. Thanks are due to the following for permission to reprint the selections below:

"New Year Letter" by W. H. Auden. Copyright © 1940.
"Starhorn" by Shirley Rousseau Murphy. From *The Unicorn Treasury* compiled by Bruce Coville. Copyright © 1987 by Shirley Rousseau Murphy. Reprinted by permission of Shirley Rousseau Murphy.
"The Unicorn" by Young, Ella, *The Horn Book Magazine,* March 1939, reprinted by permission of the Horn Book, Inc., 56 Roland St., Suite 200, Boston, MA 02129
The Beasts of Never by Georgess McHargue. Copyright © 1968, published by Bobbs-Merrill, Indianapolis, Indiana, 1968.
"Unicorn" by William Jay Smith. From *Laughing Time: Collected Nonsense* by William Jay Smith. Copyright © 1990 by William Jay Smith. Reprinted by permission of Farrar, Straus & Giroux, Inc.
The Black Unicorn by Terry Brooks. Copyright © 1987.
The Last Unicorn by Peter S. Beagle. Copyright © 1968.
Through the Looking Glass by Lewis Carroll. Copyright © 1946, published by Grosset & Dunlap, New York, New York, 1946.

SIMON & SCHUSTER BOOKS FOR YOUNG READERS
An imprint of Simon & Schuster Children's Publishing Division
1230 Avenue of the Americas, New York, New York 10020
Illustrations copyright © 1999 by Michael Hague
All rights reserved including the right of reproduction in whole or in part in any form.
SIMON & SCHUSTER BOOKS FOR YOUNG READERS is a trademark of Simon & Schuster.
Book design by Lily Malcom
The text of this book is set in Packard.
The illustrations are rendered in pen-and-ink and watercolor.
Printed in Hong Kong
10 9 8 7 6 5 4 3 2 1
Library of Congress Cataloging-in-Publication Data
Hague, Michael.
[Magical World of Unicorns]
Michael Hague's magical world of unicorns / with illustrations by Michael Hague.—1st ed.
p.   cm.
Summary: Illustrations accompany passages from poems, plays, stories, and proverbs about unicorns.
ISBN 0-689-82849-7
[1. Unicorns—Literary collections. 2. Unicorns—Literary collections.]
I. Title. II. Title: Magical world of unicorns.
PZ5.H12Mi 1999
98-31792

Michael Hague's
Magical World of Unicorns

SIMON & SCHUSTER BOOKS FOR YOUNG READERS

O Unicorn among the cedars,
To whom no magic charm can lead us . . .

— from "New Year Letter," W. H. Auden, 1940

On the edge of the world, near the end of the sea

Fairy folk gathered to dance 'neath the trees.

The sounds of their sweet-spoken musical tease

Touched the ears of the unicorn, soft as a breeze.

To the top of that mount the unicorn came;

He joined in the dance, proud and untamed.

Thrice round the circle, then hooves flashed away,

Then the trees stood alone in the light of the day.

— Ann Santinho

Run, Starhorn

Carry fire leaping from your starhorn

    Pierce worlds

    Cleft suns

    Tangle clouds

    Shatter time

      With your flaming starhorn

Bring a wish, a maiden's wish

    Head in lap

    Eyes soft

    Starhorn.

— "Starhorn,"
Shirley Rousseau Murphy, 1987

The unicorn is noble;
　　He keeps him safe and high
Upon a narrow path and steep
　　Climbing to the sky;
And there no man can take him,
　　He scorns the hunter's dart,
And only a virgin's magic power
　　Shall tame his haughty heart.

What would be now the state of us
　　But for his Unicorn,
And what would be the fate of us,
　　Poor sinners, lost, forlorn?
Oh, may He lead us on and up,
　　Unworthy though we be,
Into His Father's kingdom,
　　To dwell eternally!

— Volksleid (a popular German ballad)

Toward noon we spotted an animal gazing down at us from a sterile mountain peak of red and black rocks . . . Our guide stated that the animal must certainly be a unicorn, and he pointed out to us the single horn which jutted from its forehead. With great caution we gazed back at this most noble creature, regretting it was no closer for us to examine still more minutely.

— Friar Faber; 1438

While yet the Morning Star

Flamed in the sky

A unicorn went mincing by,

Whiter by far than blossom of the thorn:

His silver horn

Glittered as he danced and pranced

Silver-pale in the silver-pale morn.

The folk that saw him, ran away.

Where he went, so gay, so fleet,

Star-like lilies at his feet

Flowered all day,

Lilies, lilies in a throng,

And the wind made for him a song:

But he dared not stay

Over-long!

— "The Unicorn," Ella Young, 1939

Like a lion, without fear of the howling pack;

Like a gust of wind, ne'er trapped in a snare;

Like a lotus blossom, ne'er sprinkled by water;

Like me, like a unicorn, in solitude roam.

— Hymn of Buddha

The Lion-sun flies from the rising
Unicorn-moon and hides behind the
Tree or Grove of the Underworld;
the Moon pursues, and, sinking in
her turn, is sunslain.

— from *The Unicorn: A Mythological Investigation,*
Robert Brown, 1881

In the midnight forest the dark oak trees are still under the stars. The pale wildflowers in the clearing have furled their petals for the night. Suddenly he appears, a milk-white creature with the proud form of a horse. You may not notice his cloven hoofs or curling beard, but you see the curved neck, the silver mane, the graceful tail. Then he moves his head, and the moonlight runs like sea water along the pearly spiral of his horn. There is no sound, but at the next heart-beat the clearing is once again empty of all but the night.

— from *The Beasts of Never*, Georgess McHargue, 1968

To this day, it is said, malicious animals poison this water after sundown, so that none can thereupon drink it. But early in the morning, as soon as the sun rises, a unicorn comes out of the ocean, dips his horn into the water to expel the venom from it so that the other animals may drink thereof during the day. This as I describe it. I saw it with my own eyes.

— Johannes van Hesse of Utrecht; 1389

The Unicorn with the long white horn
    Is beautiful and wild.
He gallops across the forest green
So quickly that he's seldom seen
Where Peacocks their blue feathers preen
    And strawberries grow wild.
He flees the hunter and the hounds,
Upon black earth his white hoof pounds,
Over cold mountain streams he bounds
    And comes to a meadow mild;
There, when he kneels to take his nap,
He lays his head in a lady's lap
    As gently as a child.

— "Unicorn," William Jay Smith, 1957

The unicorns were the most recognizable magic the fairies possessed, and they sent them to those worlds where belief in the magic was in danger of failing altogether. After all, there has to be *some* belief in the magic—however small—for any world to survive.

— from *The Black Unicorn*, Terry Brooks, 1987

Then what is magic for? What use is wizardry if it cannot save a unicorn?

— from *The Last Unicorn*, Peter S. Beagle, 1968

"Do you know, I always thought unicorns were fabulous monsters, too? I never saw one alive before!"

"Well, now that we *have* seen each other," said the Unicorn, "if you'll believe in me, I'll believe in you."

— from *Through the Looking Glass,* Lewis Carroll, 1946

Now I will believe that there are unicorns . . .

— from *The Tempest,* William Shakespeare, 1612